This edition published by Parragon Books Ltd in 2014 and distributed by

Parragon Inc.
440 Park Avenue South, 13th Floor
New York, NY 10016
www.parragon.com

Written by Margaret Wise Brown
Illustrated by Charlotte Cooke
Designed by Kathryn Davies

ISBN 978-1-4723-6402-9

Printed in China

Wish
upon a
dream

PaRRagon

Bath · New York · Cologne · Melbourne · Delhi
Hong Kong · Shenzhen · Singapore · Amsterdam

Sleep little squirrel
and dream your dream,
Of nuts that fall and the
trickling stream.

Sleep little rabbit, the carrot grows,
In the garden and under your nose.

Sleep little horse, the day is over,
Dream of fields covered with clover.

The children dream of hammers and nails,
And spinning tops and boats with sails.

The little girl dreams of clouds up high,
And rabbits and horses that leap through the sky.

For everyone, the world is a wish,

For the child,

the rabbit,

and the fish.

Wish upon your dreams tonight,
And may your dreams last till daylight.

The honey bee dreams of busy days,
Spent making honey in the summer haze.

The fish must dream of more and more water,

Of a dolphin's niece
and a turtle's daughter.

The little bird dreams of endless song,
Sung in the branches all night long.

The little mouse dreams of another mouse,
Tucked up warm in a tiny house.

As you are falling deep into sleep,
In your heart, your hopes you keep.

So, wish upon your dreams tonight,
And may your dreams last till daylight.

Night comes along without a sound,
With soft, dark shadows all around.

Eyes and flowers all must close,

The child's,

the rabbit's,

and the rose.

Dreaming child, what you shall see,

Deep in sleep might someday be.